The Mole Sisters
and the Way Home

written and illustrated by Roslyn Schwartz

Annick Press Ltd.
Toronto • New York • Vancouver

Annick Press Ltd.
All rights reserved. No part of this work covered by the copyrights hereon may be
reproduced or used in any form or by any means – graphic, electronic, or mechanical –
without the prior written permission of the publisher.

We acknowledge the support of the Canada Council for the Arts, the Ontario
Arts Council, the Government of Ontario through the Ontario Book Publishers
Tax Credit program and the Ontario Book Initiative, and the Government of
Canada through the Book Publishing Industry Development Program (BPIDP) for
our publishing activities.

Cataloging in Publication
Schwartz, Roslyn
   The mole sisters and the way home / written and illustrated by Roslyn Schwartz.

(The mole sisters series)
ISBN 1-55037-821-X (bound).--ISBN 1-55037-820-1 (pbk.)

   I. Title. II. Series: Schwartz, Roslyn. Mole sisters series.

PS8587.C5785M648 2003   jC813'.54   C2003-901673-0
PZ7

The art in this book was rendered in colored pencils.
The text was typeset in Apollo.

Distributed in Canada by: Published in the U.S.A. by Annick Press (U.S.) Ltd.
Firefly Books Ltd.   Distributed in the U.S.A. by:
3680 Victoria Park Avenue   Firefly Books (U.S.) Inc.
Willowdale, ON   P.O. Box 1338, Ellicott Station
M2H 3K1   Buffalo, NY 14205

Printed and bound in Canada by Kromar Printing Ltd., Winnipeg, Manitoba.

visit us at: **www.annickpress.com**

Hope little Evan will enjoy 'The mole sisters' escapades in his literary years to come.

Veronika, Elvyra & Harvey Krousas

To Ma

Calgary
2011

The mole sisters were on
their way home ...

... when it started to snow.

"Aaaaah," they said.

"Oooooo."

"What fun!"

"Hey ho."

"On we go."

"What have we here?"

Squeak squeak

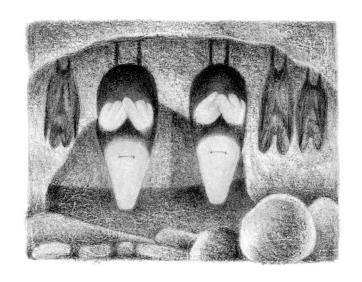

"Ups-a-daisy."

"How exciting."

"Yes indeedy."

"We've never been this way before."

"Everyone's here."

"But where are *we*?"

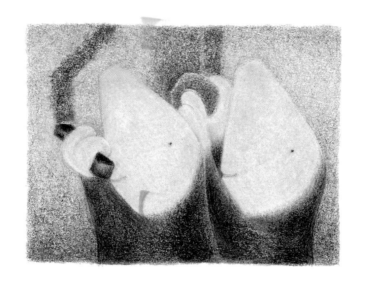

"Just a minute …"

"There we are!"

"Now on we go,"
said the mole sisters.

"Hey ho."

And on they went ...

all the way home.

Also about the Mole Sisters:

The Mole Sisters and the Rainy Day
The Mole Sisters and the Piece of Moss
The Mole Sisters and the Busy Bees
The Mole Sisters and the Wavy Wheat
The Mole Sisters and the Moonlit Night
The Mole Sisters and the Blue Egg
The Mole Sisters and the Question
The Mole Sisters and the Cool Breeze
The Mole Sisters and the Fairy Ring